SUPERMAN

DC COMICS™

SUPER HEROES

LIVEWIRE!

WRITTEN BY
BLAKE A. HOENA

ILLUSTRATED BY
DAN SCHOENING

SUPERMAN CREATED BY
~~JERRY~~ SIEGEL AND
~~JOE~~ SHUSTER

First published in this format in 2014 by Curious Fox,
an imprint of Capstone Global Library Limited,
7 Pilgrim Street, London, EC4V 6LB
– Registered company number: 6695582

www.curious-fox.com
The moral rights of the proprietor have been asserted.

CAPG33555

Art Director: Bob Lentz
Designers: Bob Lentz and Steve Mead
Production Controller: Helen McCreath
Editors: Vaarunika Dharmapala, Dan Nunn and Holly Beaumont
Originated by Capstone Global Library Ltd
Printed and bound in China by Leo Paper Group

ISBN 978 1 78202 1145 2
18 17 16 15 14
10 9 8 7 6 5 4 3 2 1

A CIP catalogue record for this book is available
from the British Library.

CONTENTS

CHAPTER 1

SHOCK JOCK

At Stryker's Island Prison, a guard patrolled a long corridor. His boots clicked loudly on the concrete floor, and his footsteps echoed down the corridor.

The hall was lined with cells designed to hold Metropolis's most dangerous criminals. The guard paused in front of each cell, making sure the criminal it imprisoned was safely inside. One of them held Rudy Jones, also known as the villainous Parasite. He could suck the energy from living things just by touching them.

Rudy was sitting on his bunk as the guard stopped in front of his cell. He looked up and asked, "What time is it?"

"Almost 9.00 a.m.," the guard replied.

"Time for the *Livewire* show," Rudy said.

"I know," the guard said. "I'll turn on the radio as soon as I get back to my desk."

"Thanks," Rudy said.

The guard turned away from Rudy and continued down the corridor. At the end of the corridor sat a desk with a small radio on it. The guard plopped down in a chair and turned on the radio. A female voice squealed across the airwaves.

"Wake up, Metropolis! This is WLXL, 95.5 Alive. It's time for *Livewire*, the only show you should have your twitchy little ears tuned to. I'm your host Leslie Willis."

Down the corridor, Rudy sat in his bunk, smiling. He leaned forwards to listen closely to what Leslie had to say.

"Turn it up," Rudy said.

The guard leaned across the desk, turning the volume knob on the radio.

"Today, I'd like to talk about one of my least favourite topics: Superman," shrieked the shock jock. "Is Superman really a hero? Or is he just a caped Boy Scout telling all the baddies where Metropolis is?

"Sure, he may have stopped Brainiac from destroying Earth. But think about it, people. How many of you ever heard of Brainiac before Superman came along? Or Metallo? Or Bizarro for that matter?

"Dare I say it?

"Not one of you!"

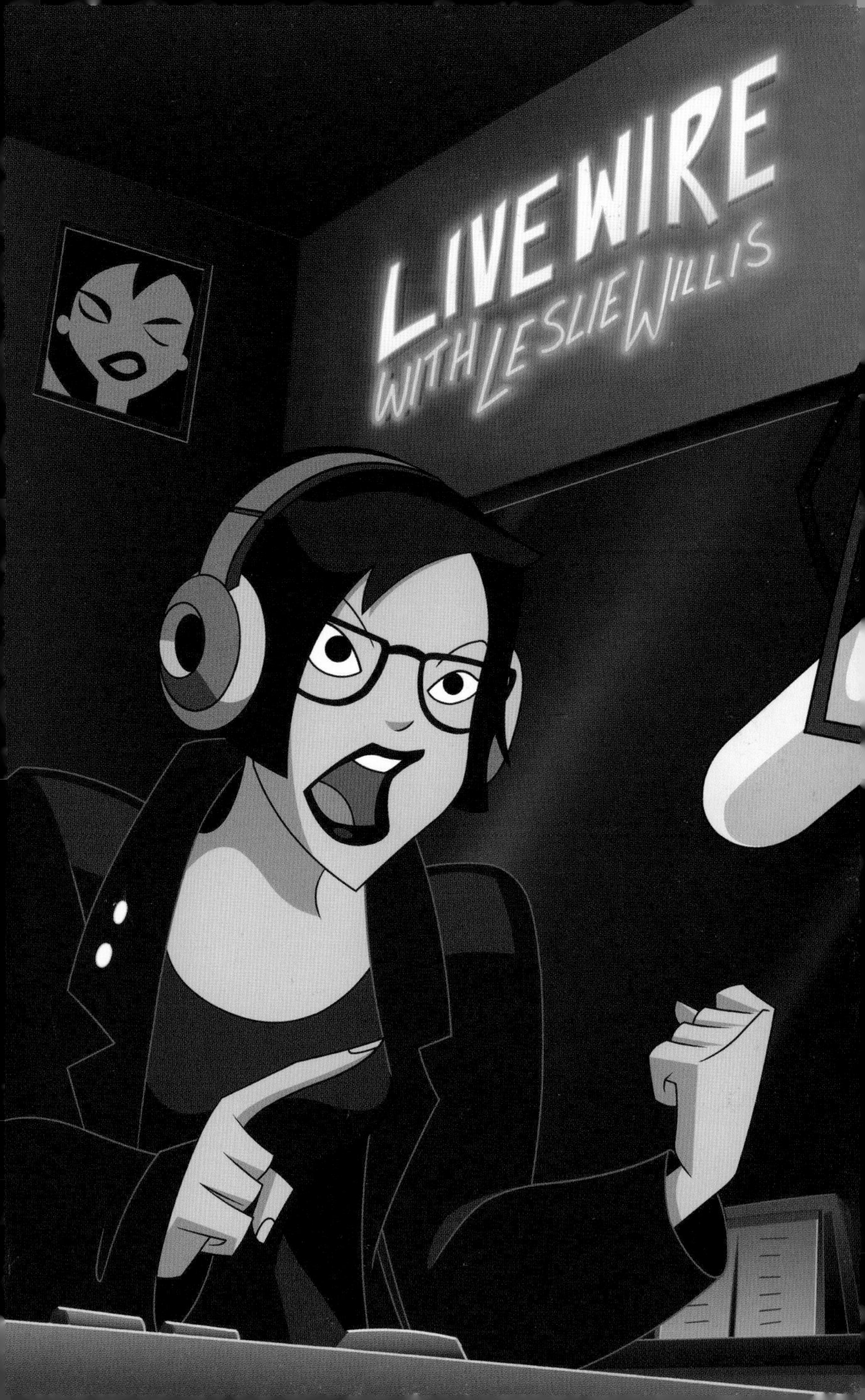
LIVE WIRE
WITH LESLIE WILLIS

"She's got a point," said Jimmy Olsen. The youthful photographer for the *Daily Planet* sat in the paper's newsroom with reporters Lois Lane and Clark Kent. They were listening to Leslie on the radio.

"Jimmy," Lois scolded. "Superman has saved your life and mine several times."

"I mean, uh, I just," Jimmy stumbled over his words, embarrassed. "Just because I listen to Willis's show doesn't mean I don't like Superman."

"Hmf!" Lois folded her arms across her chest in dismay. She added, "I can't believe people listen to this rubbish. She's just saying bad things about Superman to increase her ratings."

"Quiet," Clark said. "I want to hear what else she has to say."

"…Superman is a trouble magnet," Leslie continued. "If he wasn't polluting our skies, super-villains wouldn't give a hoot about Metropolis. For all my fans who feel the same, come down to Centennial Park tonight. I'm having a big party. We're going to celebrate my three-year dominance of the airwaves!"

Just then, Perry White, editor-in-chief of the *Daily Planet*, entered the newsroom.

"I'm glad you're such big fans of Miss Willis," Perry said. "Because I'm sending you down to Centennial Park tonight."

"But, Perry," Lois said. "Did you hear what she said about –"

"I don't care!" Perry cut her off. "This celebration will be a huge event. I want my best reporters there."

Looking at Jimmy, Perry added, "And you can take some photographs."

"Great!" Jimmy exclaimed. "Maybe I can get Leslie's autograph."

There was a long pause as everyone glared at Jimmy.

"What?" Jimmy asked. "She's popular with all the kids."

Suddenly, Perry shouted, "What're you all sitting around for? We've got a paper to run!"

A REAL SHOCKER

Later that night, at Centennial Park, Clark and Jimmy stood at the back of a large crowd. In front of them was a stage covered with lights and thumping speakers. On stage, a band played, with guitars wailing and drums pounding.

"I won't get Leslie's autograph from back here," Jimmy shouted over the noise.

Clark frowned at him.

"I mean," Jimmy said with a grin, "I won't get any good pictures."

"I think I saw Lois up near the stage," Clark said. "Why don't you try to find her?"

Jimmy shoved his way into the wall of people and quickly disappeared. Clark stayed back, keeping his eye on things. On the ground, the crowd cheered and screamed. Flickers of lightning danced among the black clouds above.

Glancing at his watch, Clark noticed that a few raindrops had dampened his sleeve. *Looks like Mother Nature isn't one of Leslie's fans* Clark thought.

Up on stage, the band ended their song, and the crowd cheered. RUMMMMMMMBLE! A deep, thunderous sound mixed with the applause. More rain fell, and more lightning flashed. The crowd kept cheering as the ground turned to mud beneath their feet.

Before the band could begin another song, a police officer stepped on to the stage. He walked up to the microphone.

"Sorry, folks," the police officer said. "There's a severe thunderstorm headed our way. We ask that everyone seek shelter. It's for your own safety. I'm afraid the show is cancelled."

Just then, Leslie walked on to the stage. Her dark eyes and darker hair were nearly as black as the overcoat she wore. She snatched the microphone from the police officer.

"It appears we have a problem, people!" Leslie shouted as she stomped around on the stage. "The cops want to shut the party down. What do you say to that?"

"Booooooo!" the crowd roared.

"Are you going to let them tell us what to do?" she asked.

"No!" the crowd screamed.

Turning towards the police officer, Leslie said, "See, what we have here is a democracy. And the people have spoken!"

Leslie held the microphone out to the crowd. "LESLIE! LESLIE! LESLIE!" they chanted wildly.

Seeing that things were turning ugly, Clark ducked into an alley. With no one around, he quickly shed his suit and tie to reveal his true identity. He was Superman, Last Son of Krypton. The rays from Earth's yellow sun gave him unimaginable powers. Superman leaped into the air and flew above the swarm of people. He zoomed towards the stage.

Meanwhile, the scene continued to grow uglier. The clouds darkened overhead, and lightning crackled in the background. People screamed and shouted as Leslie riled them up.

"Come on! Say it with me, people," Leslie yelled as the wind whipped her hair around. "We're not going to take it!"

"We're not going to take it!" the crowd echoed. "WE'RE NOT GOING TO TAKE IT!"

When Superman landed on the stage, the masses quietened down. But Leslie quickly turned on him.

"Look here, people!" Leslie sneered. "The cops brought a man in a cape."

The crowd roared with laughter.

"You're endangering these people," Superman whispered to Leslie.

"Did you hear that?" Leslie yelled to the crowd. "Ol' big blue's got his pyjamas on. He needs his beauty rest and wants everyone else to go to bed like good little boys and girls," Leslie ranted.

"What do you say to that?" Leslie asked the swarm of people.

The crowd jeered. The shock jock had turned her fans against the Man of Steel. Now they all acted just like her.

KA-BOOM! Overhead, lightning flashed. Thunder boomed.

BZZT! The microphone in Leslie's hand crackled. Buckets of rain fell, soaking everyone. Gusts of wind tore at people's clothes. Worried faces poked up in the crowd as the weather worsened, but Leslie would not stop.

"See, Superman," she screeched. "I'm the ringmaster of this circus. People listen to me. Not the TV. Not the papers. Not some muscle-bound creep in tights!"

As if on cue, lightning struck the top of the stage. **ZZAPPPPPPP!**

Lights flickered. Speakers popped. Electricity crackled everywhere.

Superman leaped in front of the lightning as it shot on to the stage. He tried to shield Leslie. Electric fingers sizzled and snapped, wrapping Superman in pale blue light.

"Arrgh!" Superman groaned in pain.

Leslie stumbled backwards, away from Superman. But she wasn't quick enough. The lightning jumped from Superman to her. She was caught in its crackling grasp.

 Leslie screamed.

Sparks covered her body. Her hair stood on end. Bolts of electricity shot out of her eyes, her fingers and her toes. She cried out in agony.

Then she collapsed.

The party was over.

CHAPTER 3

LIVEWIRE

The next day, at Metropolis General Hospital, Leslie woke up. She was lying in bed and wearing a hospital gown.

She didn't feel any pain. But she was shocked by what she saw. "What's happened to me?" she shrieked, looking down at her hands.

Leslie quickly jumped out of the hospital bed. She ran over to a mirror. Her skin was chalky white. Her black hair had turned pale blue.

"Superman!" Leslie screeched. "This is all his fault!"

THUD! THUD! Leslie pounded on the wall with her fists.

"Oooohhhhh!" she growled in anger.

KRAK! The air around Leslie came to life. It crackled with white flashes of energy. Suddenly, the TV in her room snapped on. Its screen showed an image of last night's celebration. Dark clouds loomed over a cheering crowd.

"During their confrontation," a newscaster reported, "Superman and Leslie Willis were both struck by lightning. Superman was unharmed. But Metropolis's favourite shock jock is still in the hospital."

"Wait until I get my hands on Superman!" Leslie snarled.

Angrily, Leslie held out her hands in front of her, as if she were strangling someone. Blue bolts of electricity crackled between her fingers.

"Hey, what's this?" Leslie asked, surprised. "Hmmm. Let me try something. I'm feeling a little power hungry."

She held her arms out and scrunched her face in concentration. **FzzzT!** Bolts of energy leaped from the lights and the TV, encircling Leslie. They whirled about the room, crackling and sizzling. The air was alive with electricity.

"Ooh, that feels better!" Leslie laughed.

Just then, a nurse poked his head into the room. "What's going on in here?" he asked.

"Ever hear of knocking?" Leslie snapped.

She pointed a finger at the cowering nurse. A blast of energy erupted from Leslie's hand. *BZZT!* The bolt struck the nurse. He was thrown backwards and crashed to the floor.

Seconds later, two orderlies came into the room. Leslie threw bolts of electricity at them as well. They ducked out of the way. The lightning flashed past, leaving black, smouldering scars on the wall behind them.

"Okay, kids. I'm tired of playing with you," Leslie said, placing her hands on her hips. "I have bigger fish to fry."

One second, Leslie was standing in the middle of her hospital room. The next, she was a lightning bolt of dancing energy. Blue light flickered throughout the room as she streamed, crackling and sizzling, into one of the wall outlets. Then she was gone.

Metropolis was lit by thousands of neon lights. In the city's centre, people hustled along the sidewalks. Cars beeped and honked in the streets. In the centre of it all, mounted on the side of a tall building, was a huge TV screen. It flashed images of famous celebrities and clothing ads.

KA-BOOM! A bolt of lightning erupted from one of the street lamps. As the bolt faded, Leslie appeared in its place. Still dressed in her hospital gown, she looked around, admiring the scene.

"Ahhh, Metropolis," she said. "This is my kind of town. Lights. People. Energy!"

Leslie sneered. "Especially the energy."

Leslie lifted her hands above her head. Lights flickered and popped. Bolts of energy raced from them towards Leslie.

"Ha ha," Leslie laughed. "I'm getting a charge out of this!"

People screamed as flashes of electricity flew overhead, crashing into buildings. Shards of glass from shattered windows rained down as people ran for safety. Cars squealed their tyres and raced away as chunks of concrete fell from buildings and thudded to the ground.

Soon, the streets were empty and quiet. "Hey," Leslie smirked. "Where'd everybody go? I was about to treat them to some shocking news."

"Still endangering people, I see," a voice spoke from above Leslie.

"Superman!" Leslie said with a gasp.

"I'm glad to see you're feeling better," Superman said.

"Actually, I'm feeling quite energized," Leslie replied. She pointed a finger at Superman. A blast of energy erupted from her hand, zapping him in the chest.

"Oof!" Superman grunted as he smashed into a building. Then he fell to the ground with a thud.

"You're not ruining *this* celebration, Superman," Leslie snickered. She whirled about in a flash of crackling light. Her hospital gown shimmered. Then it changed into a sleek black outfit. "And look, I even have a new party dress for the occasion!"

"I did that by electrifying the air around me," Leslie explained. "I'm pure energy now, baby!"

Superman stood up and walked over to Leslie. "Listen, Miss Willis," he began.

"Oh, and it's not Miss Willis anymore," she chuckled. She looked up at a billboard advertising her *Livewire* program. "My name is Livewire!"

"I'm just here to help," Superman said.

"I got enough help from you last night," Livewire said.

She aimed a blast of electricity at Superman. He dodged the bolt and then rushed towards her. But she was too quick. She changed into a bolt of energy. Livewire leaped into the TV overlooking the square. Suddenly, her face appeared on the screen.

"Ha, missed me, Superman! Now – lights out," Leslie laughed. "I hope you aren't afraid of the dark."

Everywhere, lights and TVs began to flicker. Then everything went dark.

CHAPTER 4

QUEEN OF ALL MEDIA

Back at the *Daily Planet* building, Lois and Jimmy sat in the dark. There was no power. A candle sputtered on Lois's desk. It gave them just enough light to work by.

Mr White approached them. He carried a typewriter. "Ah," Mr White began. "This reminds me of the good old days – back before computers and the internet were around."

"You mean," Jimmy said, making a face at the typewriter, "back when dinosaurs roamed the Earth?"

"Just because the power's out," Perry said, angrily, "doesn't mean we aren't going to put out a paper. Now get to work, you two!"

THUD! Perry slammed the typewriter down on Lois's desk. "And where's Clark?" he asked. Suddenly all of the TVs and computers throughout Metropolis snapped on. Livewire's face appeared on all of the screens.

"Good evening, citizens of Metropolis!" Livewire squealed. "This is Livewire, coming to you at a gazillion megahertz. I've restored power to all your favourite media outlets. Now you can tune in to me, queen of all media!"

"I am so sick of her," Jimmy said.

He reached over to turn off the radio.

As he did, an electric hand reached out of the radio and slapped him. **KRAK!**

"Ouch!" Jimmy yelped.

"Don't touch that dial, Metropolis," Livewire warned. "You are now my captive audience for the rest of your miserable lives!"

Miles away, in the control room of Metropolis's main power plant, Superman talked to the plant's foreman.

"I don't understand it, Superman," the foreman said. "The power is getting drained from the plant as fast as we can supply it."

"That's because there's a live wire on the other end," Superman said. "Can you shut the plant down?"

"Sure," the foreman replied, flipping switches. "It shouldn't take very long."

Throughout the power plant, machines huffed and clunked. Then the whir of the plant's generators suddenly began to grow quieter.

On the big-screen TV in central Metropolis, Livewire's face shone brightly.

"Okay, people," Livewire explained to the crowd gathered in the main square. "If you want your puny little lives to go back to normal, send me your money. All of it. Every last penny in your kiddies' piggy banks, too. From now on, I'm the media. I'm the electric company. I'm the telev –"

On the screen, Livewire's image flickered and crackled. TVs and computers in the city went blank. Radios were silent.

A large spark emerged on a power line. It sizzled and popped, speeding towards the city's main power plant.

At the power plant, the spark leaped from the power line and transformed into Livewire. She looked into the plant's control room and saw Superman.

"Oh!" she gasped. "I should have known!"

BZZT! Livewire sent a bolt of electricity towards Superman. It hit him in the back. He was sent tumbling through one of the control room's windows. Livewire zapped over to the fallen hero as plant workers scrambled for their lives.

"Must you continue to rain on my parade?" she growled.

"Sorry, Miss Willis," Superman groaned. "But this power plant is offline. You won't get any more energy here."

"I've told you before. It's not Miss Willis, it's Livewire!" she screamed.

In the blink of an eye, Leslie turned into a bolt of energy. She leaped into a nearby power line. A spark of electricity zoomed along the line and quickly disappeared.

Superman turned to the plant's foreman. "Where's the nearest source of electricity?" he asked.

"The hydroelectric plant," the nervous foreman replied. "At the dam."

Superman flew away in a flash.

CHAPTER 5

FIZZLED OUT

A large spark sizzled along a power line. It raced towards Metropolis's hydroelectric plant. Once it reached the dam, the spark entered the plant's control room. Then it leaped from the wire, landing between some workers. As the spark faded, Livewire appeared in its place. The workers screamed and ran away.

"What? Never seen a girl before?" Livewire said, laughing.

Livewire lifted her hands. The plant's generators began to whir loudly.

"Time to recharge!" Livewire squealed.

Fzzzt! Bolts of energy leaped from the generators. They streamed through Livewire. Her body was illuminated in electric light.

"Ahhhh," she said. "That feels better."

High above, Superman sped towards the plant. He flew through its entrance and burst into the control room.

"You again!" Livewire growled. "You're becoming a pest."

Superman landed in front of Livewire. "Listen, Miss Willis," he began.

Livewire's face twisted in anger. She shot a blast of electricity at Superman. The bolt of energy slammed into his chest, sending him whirling across the room. Superman crashed into a wall and fell to the floor.

"It's Livewire!" she screeched. "Can't you get it through your thick skull?"

Superman groaned and struggled back to his feet.

"Do you want some more?" she yelled.

BZZT! Livewire sent another bolt of electricity at Superman. This time, he was prepared. He held his hands out in front of him, blocking the blast. As the bolt sizzled and snapped, Superman leaned into it. He pushed his way towards Livewire. Slowly, inch by inch, he crept closer as energy exploded from her fingers.

Once he was within reach, Superman leaped forward. He grabbed Livewire's hands. The pair struggled and then tumbled to the floor. They spun towards the control room's outer wall.

When they hit the outer wall, there was a loud blast. **BANG!** The wall cracked. Chunks of concrete thudded to the ground.

Superman and Livewire rolled outside. They didn't stop until they crashed into the foot of the dam.

With a burst of energy, Livewire tossed Superman aside.

"Get away from me!" Livewire yelled. She sent a bolt of electricity at Superman. It caught him in its grasp. He was tossed backwards.

"I'm really getting tired of you," Livewire growled.

She sent bolt after bolt of electricity at Superman. As each one struck, he moaned in pain. **GROOOOAAAANNN!**

Livewire forced him backwards, until he was up against the wall of the dam.

"Now I've got you," Livewire chuckled. "And I promise, this is going to hurt!"

A large ball of energy formed in Livewire's hand. It snapped and popped loudly as she threw it at Superman.

The ball raced towards Superman at lightning speed. But he was quicker. Superman ducked the blast. **BOOM!** It exploded against the dam's cement wall, creating a gaping hole.

FWOOSHHHHH! A jet of water burst from the hole, striking Livewire. "Nooooo!" she screamed as water engulfed her.

Electricity crackled and sizzled all over Livewire's body. She screamed in pain.

The water was shorting her out. Then, with one final , the electricity in her body fizzled out. She collapsed and was carried away by the water.

With his heat vision, Superman quickly sealed the hole in the dam's wall. Once the water had stopped, he flew towards Livewire. He found her, passed out, near a shallow puddle of water.

Later that day, outside Livewire's jail cell, Superman talked with a prison guard.

"She's not going anywhere. Her cell is completely insulated," the guard explained. "Not even a spark can get in or out."

Superman looked into Livewire's cell through a thick plastic window. She slouched on her bunk. Her chin rested in the palms of her hands.

"I don't think the cell's big enough to contain her ego, though," Superman said.

The guard laughed nervously as the two of them turned from Livewire's cell and walked down the corridor.

Livewire jumped up from her bunk. She pounded on the window. BANG! BANG!

"Hey! Don't leave me in here alone," Leslie yelled.

"What am I going to do without an audience? Whom can I share my wisdom with?" Leslie pleaded.

In the cell across from her, Rudy Jones woke up.

"Hey, you're the lady from the radio," Rudy said. "I like what you have to say about Superman."

"Superman? Superman!" Leslie shrieked. "Why that caped Boy Scout! When I get my hands on him…"

WHO IS LIVEWIRE?

Leslie Willis was a radio show host known to electrify listeners with her controversial opinions. As Leslie began one of her anti-Superman rants at a live show, the Man of Steel came to warn her of an oncoming storm. As usual, she just mocked him. When lightning struck, Superman shielded Leslie as best he could, but the bolt passed through him and into her. Leslie was changed into a walking, talking spark plug – and she blames Superman for everything. As Livewire, she wants to use the Man of Steel as a lightning rod to get her revenge.

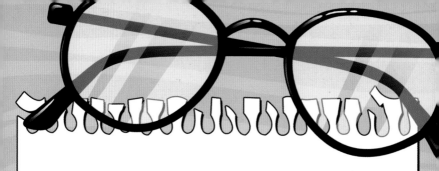

- Livewire possesses enough voltage to make her a difficult foe for the Man of Steel. Her power, while great, is not infinite – she must regularly recharge herself by sucking energy from Metropolis's power plants.

- As a radio shock jock, Leslie Willis ran wild on the airwaves of Metropolis radio. But as Livewire, she takes it a step further. She can instantly ride the airwaves – or the power lines – to anywhere in Metropolis!

- Superman seemed to have permanently short-circuited Livewire in a puddle of water. But Lex Luthor, Superman's arch-nemesis, brought the drained dynamo back to his secret lab and jolted her back to life!

- When Darkseid attacked Earth, Superman's heart stopped beating. Livewire realized that she, along with Earth itself, would be destroyed unless she revived the Man of Steel. So Livewire placed her hands on Superman's chest and gave his heart a shock, bringing him back to life and into the fight.

SUPERMAN

THE DEADLY DOUBLE

LITTLE GREEN MEN

LIVEWIRE!

PRANKSTER OF PRIME TIME

METEOR OF DOOM

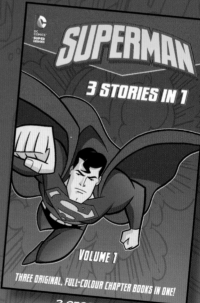

3 STORIES IN 1

Curious Fox

DC COMICS™
SUPER HEROES

BATMAN

SCARECROW, DOCTOR OF FEAR

THE FOG OF FEAR

MAD HATTER'S MOVIE MADNESS

THE REVENGE OF CLAYFACE

BATMAN

3 Stories in 1

Volume 1

THREE ORIGINAL, FULL-COLOUR CHAPTER BOOKS IN ONE!

3 STORIES IN 1

ROBIN'S FIRST FLIGHT

Curious Fox

MYSTERIES

Solve a mystery with Scooby-Doo!

**SCOOBY-DOO AND
THE GROOVY GHOST**

**SCOOBY-DOO AND
THE KARATE CAPER**

**SCOOBY-DOO AND
THE SUNKEN SHIP**

**SCOOBY-DOO AND
THE VAMPIRE'S REVENGE**

For more exciting books
from brilliant authors,
follow the fox!

www.curious-fox.com

Curious Fox